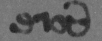

I'm a Little Teapot

I'm a Little Teapot

As told and illustrated by
Iza Trapani

🐾 Whispering Coyote
A Charlesbridge Imprint

A special "thank you" to Emma, Max, and Mick
for their wonderful suggestions.

A Whispering Coyote Book
Book and illustrations copyright © 1996 by Whispering Coyote Press L.P.
All rights reserved, including the right of reproduction in whole or in part in any form. Charlesbridge,
Whispering Coyote, and colophon are registered trademarks of Charlesbridge Publishing, Inc.

"I'm A Little Teapot" written by Clarence Kelley and George Sanders
Copyright © 1939 Kelman Music Corporation
Copyright renewed 1967 by Marilyn Sanders O'Bradovich
International copyright secured. All rights reserved.
Adaptation by Iza Trapani © 1996 Marilyn Sanders O'Bradovich

Published by Charlesbridge
85 Main Street
Watertown, MA 02472
(617) 926-0329
www.charlesbridge.com

Library of Congress Cataloging-in-Publication Data
Trapani, Iza.
I'm a little teapot / adapted & illustrated by Iza Trapani.
p. cm.
Summary: Expanded verses of a familiar song tell how a teapot dreams of visiting China, Mexico,
the opera, a jungle, and other places while waiting to be used to serve tea.
ISBN 1-978085-99-2 (reinforced for library use)
ISBN 1-58089-010-5 (softcover)
1. Children's songs—Texts. [1. Teapots—-Songs and music. 2. Songs.] I. Title.
PZ8.3.T686   Iae 1996
782.42164'0268—dc20
[E]   96-6283
CIP   AC

Printed in China
(hc) 10 9 8 7 6 5 4
(sc) 10 9 8 7 6 5 4

Text was set in 18-point Tiffany Medium.
Book production and design by *The Kids at Our House*

For Jeannie, Laura, and Teri,
"friends forever!"
Love,
Iza

I'm a little teapot, short and stout.
Here is my handle, here is my spout.
When I get all steamed up, hear me shout.
Just tip me over, pour me out!

I'm a little teapot, come see me.
Oh how I'd love your company.
Sitting on the stove top patiently,
I wait for someone to make tea.

I'm a little teapot, I'll show you
All of the things that I'd like to do.
It's a game I play the whole day through.
Now let me share my dreams with you.

I'm a little teapot, on that note
We're off to China—grab your coat.
We can fly a kite and row our boat
And eat with chopsticks as we float.

I'm a little teapot, si señor.
All over Mexico we can tour.
I'll become a mighty matador
And fight the bull while you keep score.

I'm a little teapot, watch me fly
Just like a spaceship in the sky.
On another planet way up high,
We'll meet an alien eye to eye.

I'm a little teapot, la, la, la!
Let's take a trip to the opera.
You can sing a lovely aria,
And I'll play in the orchestra.

I'm a little teapot, hey let's play
Pirates at sea on a windy day.
Back and forth our sailing ship will sway.
Ahoy my mateys! Find the way!

I'm a little teapot, tally ho!
Off on a fox hunt we will go.
Racing with the hounds, our trumpets blow.
Now where on earth did that fox go?

I'm a little teapot, peekaboo!
Deep in the jungle I'll hide with you.
You can try to find me, if you do—
Then you can hide and I'll find you.

I'm a little teapot, golly gee!
Thank you for sharing my dreams with me.
Now I'd really like to make some tea
For all your friends and family.

I'm a little teapot, short and stout.
Here is my handle, here is my spout.
Tip me over gently, pour me out
For that's what tea time's all about!

I'm a Little Teapot

I'm a lit - tle tea - pot, short and stout. Here is my han - dle,

here is my spout. When I get all steamed up,

hear me shout. Just tip me ov - er, and pour me out!

1. I'm a little teapot, short and stout.
   Here is my handle, here is my spout.
   When I get all steamed up, hear me shout.
   Just tip me over, pour me out!

2. I'm a little teapot, come see me.
   Oh how I'd love your company.
   Sitting on the stove top patiently,
   I wait for someone to make tea.

3. I'm a little teapot, I'll show you
   All of the things that I'd like to do.
   It's a game I play the whole day through.
   Now let me share my dreams with you.

4. I'm a little teapot, on that note
   We're off to China—grab your coat.
   We can fly a kite and row our boat
   And eat with chopsticks as we float.

5. I'm a little teapot, si señor.
   All over Mexico we can tour.
   I'll become a mighty matador
   And fight the bull while you keep score.

6. I'm a little teapot, watch me fly
   Just like a spaceship in the sky.
   On another planet way up high,
   We'll meet an alien eye to eye.

7. I'm a little teapot, la, la, la!
   Let's take a trip to the opera.
   You can sing a lovely aria,
   And I'll play in the orchestra.

8. I'm a little teapot, hey let's play
   Pirates at sea on a windy day.
   Back and forth our sailing ship will sway.
   Ahoy my mateys! Find the way!

9. I'm a little teapot, tally ho!
   Off on a fox hunt we will go.
   Racing with the hounds, our trumpets blow.
   Now where on earth did that fox go?

10. I'm a little teapot, peekaboo!
    Deep in the jungle I'll hide with you.
    You can try to find me, if you do—
    Then you can hide and I'll find you.

11. I'm a little teapot, golly gee!
    Thank you for sharing my dreams with me.
    Now I'd really like to make some tea
    For all your friends and family.

12. I'm a little teapot, short and stout.
    Here is my handle, here is my spout.
    Tip me over gently, pour me out
    For that's what tea time's all about!